The Ghost
of Shadow Vale

The Ghost

of Shadow Vale

JONATHAN STROUD

With illustrations by
Siku

Barrington Stoke

First published in 2009 in Great Britain by
Barrington Stoke Ltd
18 Walker Street, Edinburgh, EH3 7LP

www.barringtonstoke.co.uk

This edition first published 2014

Text © 2009 Jonathan Stroud
Illustrations © 2009 Siku

A CIP catalogue record for this book is available
from the British Library upon request

ISBN: 978-1-78112-423-9

Printed in China by Leo

For Edward, Henry and Harvey, with love.

Contents

Chapter 1

The Haunted Valley

This is something that happened in Iceland way back. People still talk of it, but rarely after dark.

In the north of the country there was a long, deep valley that ran from the hills down to the sea. In winter the sun never reached the bottom of the valley, so it was called the Shadow Vale. A farmer named Thorhall lived here with his wife and household. He was a rich man who owned a large flock of sheep, but he was unlucky too, because the valley was haunted by a monster.

One day Thorhall went to see a friend of his, Skapti the Lawgiver.

"I need some help, Skapti," he said.

"What's the problem?" Skapti asked.

"I can't find anyone willing to be my shepherd," Thorhall said, scratching at his beard. "We've had trouble high up in the valley. There's something wicked up there, hiding among the rocks and stones. Men have come back injured, goggle-eyed, scared almost to death. They've packed and left, without a word, and now my sheep are roaming free up on the hill."

Skapti looked into the fire and thought for a moment. "Here's my advice," he said. "See what you think. I know a fellow named Glam. He came here from Sweden last year. I've never met anyone stronger or more stubborn. He won't be put off by talk of ghosts or trolls. He needs a job too, but I warn you that he's not the nicest man around."

"That doesn't bother me," Thorhall said. He stood up. "How can I find him?"

"He's up on the hillside, collecting wood," Skapti said. "You'll know him when you see him."

Thorhall set off up the hill. It wasn't long before he saw a man coming towards him, carrying a huge bundle of twigs and branches. Right away, Thorhall began to wonder whether he should forget his plan, because there was something odd about the look of the stranger. He was almost seven feet tall, with a chest like a beer barrel and great strong arms. His head was huge, with eyes as dark as slate and a shock of hair streaked grey like a wolf's skin.

The two men stopped and stared at each other.

"I'm looking for someone named Glam," Thorhall said.

The tall man said nothing. His eyes seemed to pierce the farmer through.

"I've a job to offer him," Thorhall went on. "If he wants it, that is."

"My name is Glam," the man said. "And I'm not afraid of work, if my terms are met."

"What are your terms?" Thorhall asked, feeling nervous.

"That no one bothers me," Glam said. He turned and spat on the stones beside him. "I don't like people getting in my way."

"That's fine by me," Thorhall said. "I need a shepherd, but I should tell you that the hill above my farm is haunted."

Glam laughed, showing his teeth. "It'll take more than old wives' tales to put me off," he said. "Anyway, I find ghosts better company than most men."

Chapter 2

The Wicked Shepherd

Thorhall struck a bargain with Glam, and he came to live in the household at Shadow Vale. He was a good shepherd, but no one liked him. He was rude and aggressive, and on Sundays he refused to set foot in the church with the rest of the workers. Still, Thorhall didn't mind because Glam seemed to be having no trouble up in the valley.

Winter set in and Christmas came. On Christmas Eve, it was the custom for the household to fast. No one would eat anything out of respect for the holy day to come. But Glam went to Thorhall's wife and sat down at the table.

"Don't give me your nonsense," he said. "I'm hungry and I'll be fed. Get me my breakfast, or you'll regret it."

Thorhall's wife was terrified and brought him some food. Glam ate without another word, then he went out, slamming the door behind him.

All that day the weather grew worse. It was pitch black outside and the snow fell thick and fast. The people in Thorhall's farm could hear Glam far off, calling the sheep, but in the afternoon a blizzard set in and his voice was drowned out by the howling wind.

In the evening everyone went to church. When they came back to the farm, walking bent over against the driving snow, they found that Glam had still not returned. The weather was so bad that no one went to search for him.

The night passed. Glam did not come back.

On Christmas morning, the snow lay thick upon the roof-tops and piled high against the barns and the rocks on the hills. Thorhall's sheep could be seen scattered all across the mountain. After Mass, a search party set out to look for the shepherd. They soon found signs of a titanic battle. Over a wide area the snow had been churned up, rocks had been uprooted and clods of frozen earth had been ripped from the hillside. Splashes of blood were everywhere.

The men crept closer. At last, behind a rock in the centre of the devastation, they found Glam. He was stone dead, with his body swollen, his skin crusted with ice and his wolfish eyes open, glaring at the sky.

All around Glam's body were huge footprints wider than a man's chest. They led off up the valley, alongside a trail of blood. It was clear to everyone that Glam had fought with the monster that haunted the valley, and that he had wounded it.

Thorhall's men took hold of Glam's massive body and tried to drag it down to the church. But the corpse was so heavy that no one could shift it. They brought some oxen and tied Glam's feet to the harness, but they still couldn't pull him very far.

The next day, a priest came out with the men to perform a burial service up on the

hill. Oddly, while the priest was with the men, Glam could not be found, no matter how hard anyone looked. In the end, the priest returned to the church and as soon as he had gone, Glam's body was found again. After this, everyone was keener than ever to get rid of the unholy corpse. So, without wasting any time, they buried Glam under a great heap of stones and went away.

Chapter 3

Glam's Return

Perhaps Glam gave the monster of the valley its death wound, because it was never heard of again. But it wasn't long before a much greater evil began to trouble the farm. One night, people came running to Thorhall in terror.

"We've seen him!" they cried. "Walking in the fields! He's come back!"

"Who?" Thorhall asked.

"It's him!" they said. "There's no mistaking him! We saw his eyes shining, heard his teeth snapping in the dark. He's prowling round the farm, looking for a way in!"

"Who?" Thorhall shouted, although he knew only too well.

"I saw his face in the light of the window!" one man said. "Blue with cold and crazed with hunger. I saw him – Glam!"

"Glam's dead," Thorhall spat.

"He's dead all right," they said. "But he's come back."

That was when the haunting began. Every night, all through the winter, Glam appeared at the farm. He walked among the buildings, knocking on the walls, peering

through windows and pushing on doors until the people inside heard the wood crack. He climbed onto the roof and sat there, banging his heels so hard against the turf that the whole place shook.

Soon, Glam began to appear during the short, dark mid-winter days too. People were terrified. Some fainted, some went mad and others left the valley altogether. These were hard times for Thorhall and his family.

In spring, the hauntings lessened and things were quiet over the summer. But the following winter, Glam returned. His visits grew more frequent and became more violent. Things came to a head on Christmas Eve, a year to the day after Glam had died. Thorhall's new shepherd, a man named Erlend, was about to go out to tend to the sheep when Thorhall's wife stopped him.

"Please don't go," she said. "Stay inside with us. I fear that bad things may repeat themselves today."

Erlend laughed. "It would have to be something pretty dramatic to stop me coming back," he said. "Don't worry yourself. I shall see you later in church."

So Erlend went out, and Erlend did not come back. They found him the next day, stretched out on the stones of Glam's grave. Every bone in his body was broken.

From then on, Glam's activities went from bad to worse and spread all along the valley. No one in any farm was safe. More of Thorhall's men were killed and so were many of his animals. In the end, everyone apart from Thorhall, his wife and a few loyal servants abandoned the farm for the winter and fled down to the coast. All the nearby farms were left deserted. Everyone in that part of Iceland lived in fear of their lives and no one had any idea what to do.

Chapter 4

The Strongest Man in Iceland

No one was more interested in what was going on in Shadow Vale than a man called Grettir Asmundarson. He was the strongest man living in the country, and a very great hero. Grettir was often heard to say that he could beat any three warriors in battle whenever he chose, and that four warriors wouldn't be out of the question. Grettir proved his words true several times over, for he was quick to protect his friends from arrogant neighbours and even quicker to avenge any insult to his honour. He had killed many men in different disputes and people became very wary of taking him on.

No one dared say anything bad about Grettir, but some men shook their heads whenever his name came up. "He's a great fighter, all right," they muttered into their ale, "but is he lucky? He's not frightened of anything, and is too head-strong for his own good. He never knows when to stop and think things over. Every time he kills an enemy, he makes ten more, because all the dead man's relatives swear revenge. If Grettir carries on like this, he'll soon have half of Iceland against him."

But Grettir didn't care. Nothing seemed too difficult for him and his worst problem was that he was often bored. He was eager for a real challenge that would test his strength.

It so happened that Grettir's uncle Jokul lived at the end of Shadow Vale, and Grettir went to visit him.

"Tell me," Grettir said, "are the stories that I've been hearing really true? This Glam seems to have got everyone tied up in knots!"

"It's no laughing matter, nephew," Jokul replied. "This must be the worst haunting that I can remember. Glam is more wicked than any other ghost and if, as I suspect, you're thinking of poking your nose into the affair, take my advice – stay well away! This is a very different matter to bashing a few heads together."

"Maybe, but I might just call in on Shadow Vale anyway," Grettir said. "I've heard the scenery is good up there."

His uncle Jokul leaned forward and grasped Grettir's arm. "Listen," he said. "All our family has high hopes of you. We don't want to see you waste the gifts you were born with. Believe me, if there's one sure way of bringing ill luck down on your head, it's tangling with evil spirits. Nothing good can come from them. Stay here with me for the winter. Many of my friends have very pretty daughters who are on the look-out for a man like you. We can visit them and see what you think."

Grettir shook his head. "I've no interest in chasing girls while our neighbours are being murdered," he said. "And nor should you. It could be your farm that Glam visits next. Thank you for your offer, Uncle, but

I will set off early tomorrow and see what Thorhall has to say for himself."

"Do what you must," Jokul said sadly. "I'll say no more."

Chapter 5

Staying the Night

The next day, Grettir rode up the valley to Thorhall's farm. When Thorhall saw Grettir, he went out to greet him.

"Where are you going?" he asked.

"I was wondering if I could stay with you tonight," Grettir said, and he got down from his horse.

Thorhall looked surprised. "Of course, if you wish," he said, "but perhaps you don't know where you are. I wouldn't want you to suffer on my account, so I may as well tell you that both you and your horse are at risk if you remain here."

"A new horse is easily bought," said Grettir.

With this, Thorhall welcomed Grettir to his farm. They led the horse into the stable, locked the door and went into the house. That night, everyone slept soundly. Glam did not appear.

In the morning Thorhall went out to check the horse, but all was well. The farmer was pleased, but baffled. "I don't know how you did it," he said. "That's the first time we've been left alone for months."

"Maybe Glam's changed his ways," Grettir said. "Or maybe he hasn't. I think I might stay here another night, if you don't mind."

Thorhall was happy to agree. The day passed and night came. Everyone went to bed. In the morning nothing seemed to have happened, but when Thorhall and Grettir went out to the stable they found that the door had been broken, the stalls smashed and the horse torn to pieces.

"What did I tell you?" Thorhall moaned. "We are cursed! It will never end! Well, my friend, you've lost your horse, but there's no need to lose your life as well. Set off on foot now. You'll be well away from this wretched place by dusk."

Grettir was looking at the remains of his horse. "I'm not going without payment for my loss," he said. "The least that ghost can

do is give me a good look at him in return. No, I shall stay here again tonight and see if I can meet him."

Thorhall didn't know whether to laugh or cry. "It is a great blessing that you are willing to stay and keep us company," he said, "but I warn you that no good has ever come from meeting Glam. Still, if that's what you want to do –"

Grettir slapped Thorhall on the back. "Let's go and get some breakfast," he said.

Chapter 6

Waiting for Glam

Thorhall and Grettir spent the day talking together. Outside it slowly grew dark. At last everyone went to bed, apart from Grettir. He sat quietly in the middle of the room beside the dwindling fire.

Grettir looked about him. There were plenty of signs in the house of damage caused by Glam. The main door had been broken off its hinges and had been replaced with a simple board. One of the crossbeams above the door had been split almost in two.

All the people of Thorhall's household were tucked up in their beds. Everything was very quiet. A torch was burning on the wall. Grettir got up and went over to a sturdy bench facing the door. He lay down on it and covered himself from head to toe with a thick fur cloak. He arranged it so that he could peep out through a tiny gap in the fur, and he kept his eyes fixed on the broken door.

The fire burned low, and the room grew cold. Grettir began to shiver under the cloak. Once or twice he heard snores from Thorhall's bed, but otherwise it was very still. He watched the light flicker and dim.

All at once there was a loud clatter from outside, as if a metal bucket had been kicked hard among the stones of the yard.

Then there was a great thud as something heavy landed on the roof. Grettir listened hard. He heard slow, dragging footsteps climbing the roof to the centre beam, then a thunderous banging as something began to beat its heels furiously against the turf. Flakes of bark and dirt fell from the ceiling like heavy snow. The cracked beam above the door sagged a little more. The whole hall shook.

After a long while the banging stopped. Grettir listened to the slow, dragging footsteps climbing down the roof to the edge. There was a muffled impact as heavy feet landed on the ground, and then Grettir heard them shuffling round towards the door of the house. Grettir remained very still under his cloak.

Something pushed against the door, and the stout beam that held it shut snapped like a twig. The door opened. In peered

Glam's head, as big as that of an ox or a horse. Glam's face was swollen to a colossal size, the skin was mottled white and blue, the eyes stared from their sockets.

Slowly, Glam squeezed through the door into the hall. He was still wearing the tunic and leggings he had worn on the day he died, but they were ragged and torn, the pale flesh swelling through. Once inside, Glam stood upright. He was so tall that his streaked grey hair crackled against the rafters.

Glam moved his great heavy head from side to side, scanning the room. As he looked, he ground his teeth together, making a noise like a metal blade being dragged against a rock. He stretched out a huge hand to where the torch hung on the wall. His fingers cupped the end of the burning torch and snuffed the light out.

Now the room was dark, apart from a little moonlight shining in through the doorway. Grettir could hardly see where Glam was. He felt a terrible urge to get up, to cry out and run, but he forced himself to remain as still as a stone under the cloak. In the blackness, he heard a slow movement, heard the scraping of Glam's teeth coming nearer and nearer. Grettir stayed dead still.

Two great eyes shone in the dark above him.

Chapter 7

The Fight

Glam saw the big bundle of fur lying on the bench. He bent down and reached out to pick the bundle up. Grettir felt a grip like iron on the fur cloak. He pressed his feet against the side of the bench and made himself rigid, hanging onto the cloak from beneath it.

Glam pulled at the cloak. Nothing happened – the cloak stayed where it was.

Glam pulled once more. Still the cloak didn't move. Grettir hung on with all his might, gritting his teeth with the effort. Glam tried again, and this time he wrenched at the cloak so hard that Grettir was dragged up off the bench and onto his feet.

The cloak ripped in two. Glam staggered back, and as he did so Grettir leaped forwards, ducked under Glam's swinging arms and grabbed him around his waist. He tried to knock Glam off balance so that he would fall. But Glam clutched at Grettir's arms in order to twist him loose and, locked together like this, they careered around the dark hall, crashing into benches and splintering them to match-wood.

Grettir had never felt anything as strong as the cold fingers now digging into his flesh. The terrible grip tightened. It began to force him downwards, hoping to crush him against the earth. Grettir's legs

were buckling. He stumbled backwards towards the fireplace. Over the hearth-stones and through the red-hot embers they went – Glam pushing, Grettir in retreat. Red sparks exploded up into the darkness from each impact of their scuffling feet.

When they were beyond the fireplace, Grettir exerted all his strength. He braced his feet and twisted, swinging Glam round and slamming him hard into the roof post in the centre of the hall. The post split down the middle. One of the rafters fell, and pieces of turf fell with it. But Glam remained standing. His grip on Grettir's neck did not falter.

Then, without warning, Glam stepped backwards and began to pull Grettir towards the doorway, seeking to drag him outside.

Grettir knew that if he was brought out into the open, Glam's power would overcome him. He tried to jam his feet against anything he passed – tables, posts and benches – but each time Glam pulled so hard that Grettir was forced forwards against his will.

Now Grettir was in desperate straits, for his strength was almost at an end. But he had one final trick to try. Just before they arrived at the doorway, when Glam was pulling him with all his might, Grettir suddenly stopped resisting. Instead, Grettir threw himself forwards, ramming his body against Glam's chest.

Taken by surprise, Glam toppled backwards, and fell heavily against the beam above the door. The beam split in two and the roof burst open above it. Glam and Grettir crashed through the doorway in a shower of splintered wood and roof turf. Glam landed on a jagged rock with an

impact that snapped his back in two. And Grettir landed on Glam.

Then the moon broke through a hole in the clouds. A beam of light bathed the two fighters, and Glam's eyes shone up at the moon full of wickedness and hate. At this sight, Grettir's legs turned to mush, and the strength in his arms ebbed away. He could not draw his sword, he could not move. Grettir was swallowed by a haze of fear as he lay there upon the body of Glam.

As if in a dream, Grettir heard the voice of Glam speaking to him.

"Well, Grettir," it said. "I cannot say I am pleased to have met you, but I shall make sure that you also regret meeting me. I have fallen, but I still have the power to curse you, and this I will do. Tonight you are strong, but you are only half as strong as you would have become if you had left me alone. And what is more, your strength, which has always brought you fame, will bring you nothing but bad luck from now on. I see you being forced away from the warmth of people's homes, to dwell by yourself in lonely places, a fugitive from men. And each night, while you cower alone in the darkness, you shall feel my eyes watching you, so that you are driven mad with terror. And this terror will kill you at the last."

At that moment, the moon went in behind a cloud. The light in Glam's eyes went out and his voice faded. Grettir felt the strength return to his limbs. He got up, drew his sword and cut off Glam's head.

Chapter 8

Victory?

Grettir heard a small noise behind him. Thorhall was peeping out of the shattered doorway. When Thorhall saw Grettir holding Glam's severed head, he stepped out boldly. He loudly thanked God and praised Grettir for his victory.

Grettir said little, but ordered the farmer to prepare a great bonfire. That very night they burned Glam's body. As

dawn broke, they swept the ashes up into a sack, which they carried away and buried in a remote place. Then they returned to the farm. Grettir slept all day.

When news got out about the fight, Grettir's fame spread across all of Iceland. He was called the bravest man alive, and he was showered with gifts by the people of the district.

But Grettir didn't celebrate that much. When Thorhall offered him anything that he owned, Grettir said, "A new horse would be good. And maybe some new clothes. My clothes are a bit torn." Beyond that, Grettir was not much interested in his reward.

For the fact was that some of Glam's words had already come true. Grettir didn't like being on his own at night. He saw shadows and shapes lurking on the edge of his vision, and he felt that he was being watched.

And ever afterwards, though he slew robbers, killed trolls and giants, and did many other astonishing deeds, the curse of the ghost of Shadow Vale hung over Grettir Asmundarson. To the end of his life, the strongest man in Iceland remained afraid of the dark.

Our books are tested
for children and young people by
children and young people.

Thanks to everyone who consulted on
a manuscript for their time and effort in
helping us to make our books better
for our readers.

More from *Barrington Stoke* ...

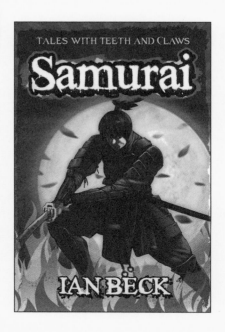

Night after night, the evil demon comes to the village. One by one, it kills the village girls.

Now samurai has come to take on the demon. The samurai has nothing to lose, and everything to prove.

He has fount and won before ... but can he win this time? Get ready for a nightmare to remember!

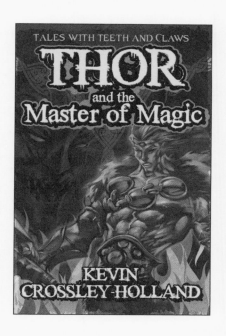

The Giants are tricksters and cheats. The Giants would like nothing better than to attack ...

Now Thor has come to take on the Giant King. Thor is strong and brave, and he is the God of Thunder. Are Thor and his hammer a match for the Master of Magic?

www.barringtonstoke.co.uk

More from *Barrington Stoke*...

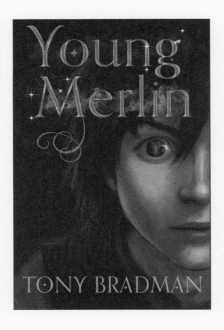

In a time of myth and a land of magic, one boy will shape the future ...

Merlin has always known he's different from the other boys. But he has no idea just how different. Inside Merlin, lies power.

Magic.

And that makes him a threat to the King ...

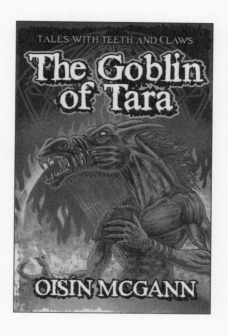

Every Halloween, the goblin creeps in from the
Otherworld. Every Halloween, flesh burns and
bodies fall.

The people of Tara need a hero. Step up Finn
MacCool. He's the only hope they've got ...

www.barringtonstoke.co.uk